Muddigush

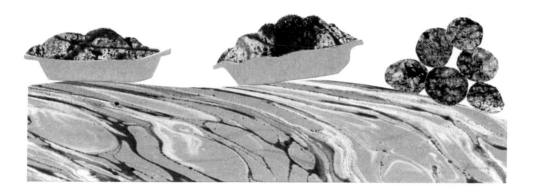

Muddigush

by Kimberley Knutson

MACMILLAN PUBLISHING COMPANY
NEW YORK

MAXWELL MACMILLAN CANADA
TORONTO

MAXWELL MACMILLAN INTERNATIONAL
NEW YORK   OXFORD   SINGAPORE   SYDNEY

This book is dedicated to:

Mom, Dad, Craig, Bruce, and Suzanne

and to those who enjoy a good romp in the mud.

Special thanks to:
The Dolphins of '88 and Kitah Gimel of '89 for their inspiration,
Jinny and Red for the first studio, Omar for his confidence,
E. Tsang for her interest and Michael Merry Christmas
for his optimism and advice.

Macmillan Publishing Company, 866 Third Avenue, New York, NY 10022

Maxwell Macmillan Canada, Inc., 1200 Eglinton Avenue East, Suite 200, Don Mills, Ontario M3C 3N1

Macmillan Publishing Company is part of the Maxwell Communication Group of Companies.

First edition
Printed in Hong Kong

10   9   8   7   6   5   4   3   2   1

The text of this book is set in 16 pt. Usherwood Medium.
The illustrations are rendered in collage.

Library of Congress Cataloging-in-Publication Data
Knutson, Kimberley.
Muddigush / by Kimberley Knutson. — 1st ed.
     p.   cm.
Summary: Describes the squishy sensations associated with playing in the mud.
ISBN 0-02-750843-9
[1. Mud—Fiction.   2. Play—Fiction.]   I. Title.
PZ7.K7864Mu   1992   [E]—dc20   91-15393

Listen!

Listen!

Listen to the rain

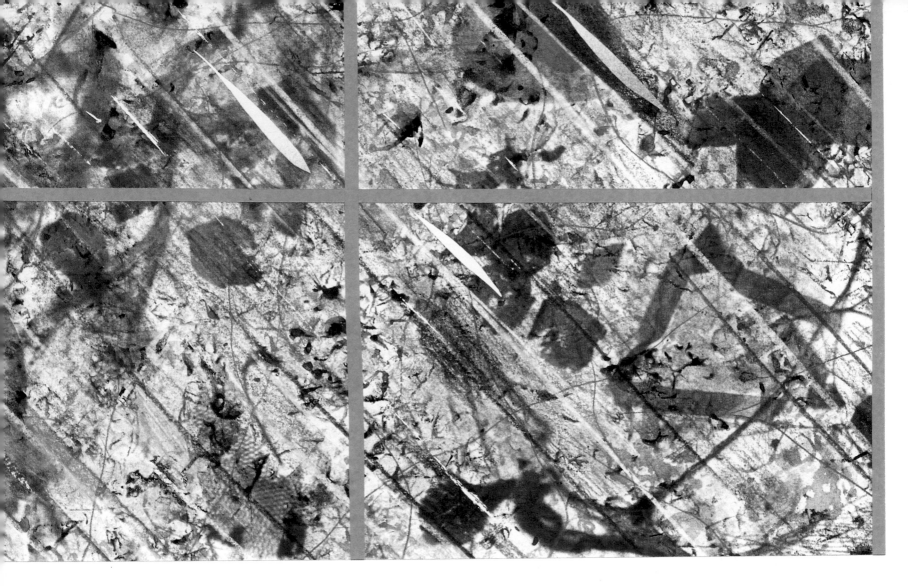

rushing

snapping

hushing…

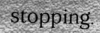

stopping.

Now outside splashing and stomping

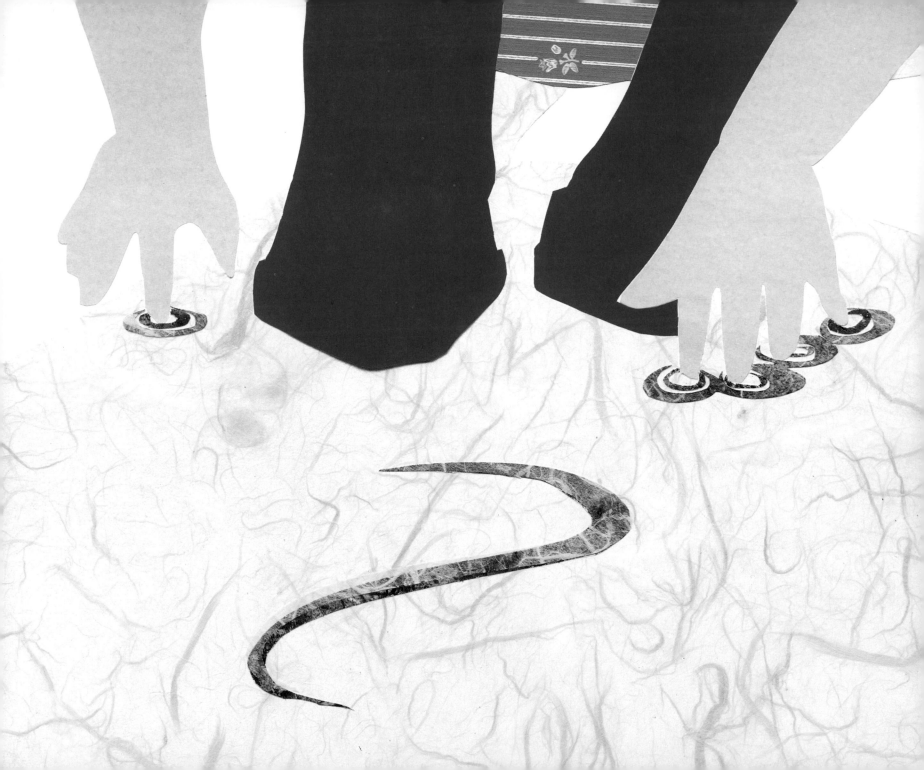

we watch the water make rivers in the skoosh and the goosh
on the ground.

Skoosh slush

goosh gush

icky sticky muddigush!

That sludgy mudge
grabs at our boots
making squelchy slimy smucky sounds.
Smucky mush
Smacky mush
Squooshy slooshy muddigush!

There's pastry to roll,

mudballs to make,

mashpies and mudlucious cakes to bake.

Stomping and stirring
we churn the sloosh
that we pull and push
with our sticks.
Smack the rivers!
Foam the bubbles!
…in the
smucky mush
smacky mush
squooshy slooshy muddigush!

Mountains to build,
new rivers to dig,
wagons to push,
and buckets to carry.

Scoop up the slime!

Pour out the puddle juice!

And shout from the slosh:

Smucky mush!

Smacky mush!

Squooshy slooshy muddigush!

The riverbed slime

is shivery and quivery,

bubbly and wiggly,

cold and jiggly.

Spread it, pat it,

till it's shiny and flat.

Smack and whack that

smucky mush

smacky mush

squooshy slooshy muddigush!

We splash the water
into our river
over and over and over.
It always disappears.

Too soon the water sinks down,
brown bubbles break,
the gush is crust,
the slippery is crumbly.
The squoosh and the goosh
are gone.

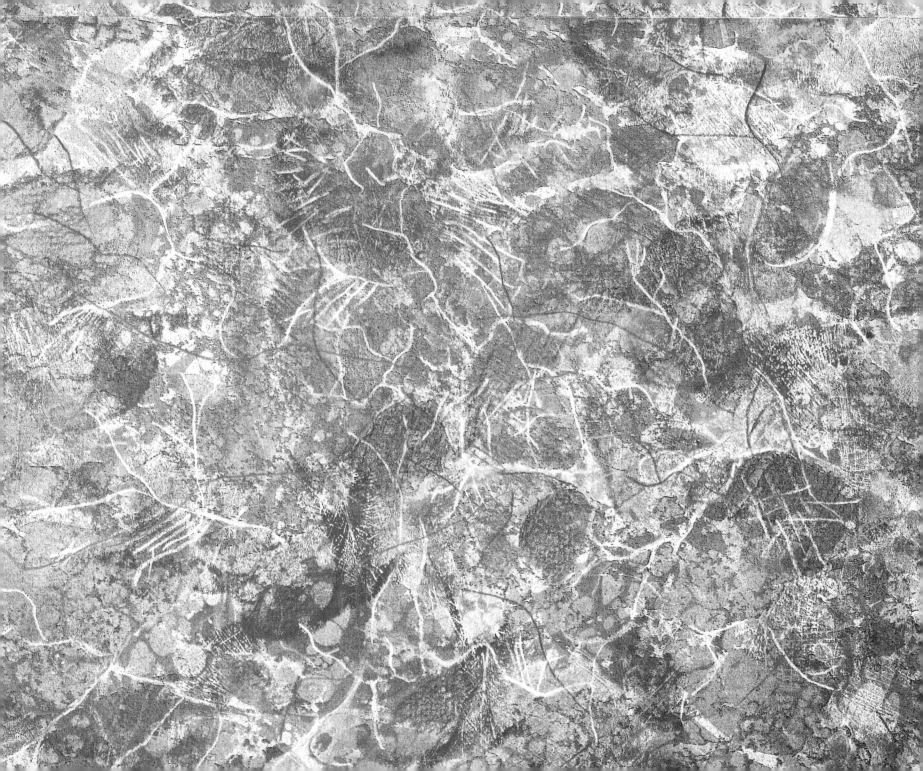

No more
smucky mush
smacky mush
squooshy slooshy muddigush.

Inside,

the slicker slides off.

Muddigush washes clean
and the water turns black
as it gurgles
and slurgles
and snurgles
down the drain.